KT-493-683

# FLEATECTIVES
## CASE OF THE MISSING GLOW-WORMS

Look out for more

# FLEATECTIVES

adventures

## CASE OF THE STOLEN NECTAR

SCHOLASTIC
FLEATECTIVES
CASE OF THE MISSING GLOW-WORMS
JONNY ZUCKER
ILLUSTRATED BY CHRIS JEVONS

First published in the UK in 2014 by Scholastic Children's Books
An imprint of Scholastic Ltd
Euston House, 24 Eversholt Street
London, NW1 1DB, UK
Registered office: Westfield Road, Southam, Warwickshire, CV47 0RA
SCHOLASTIC and associated logos are trademarks and/
or registered trademarks of Scholastic Inc.

Text copyright © Jonny Zucker, 2014
Illustrations copyright © Chris Jevons, 2014

The right of Jonny Zucker and Chris Jevons to be identified as the
author and illustrator of this work has been asserted by them.

Cover illustration © Chris Jevons, 2014

ISBN 978 1 407 13695 0

A CIP catalogue record for this book is available from the British Library.

Print

For everyone at
Fleansbrook Junior School

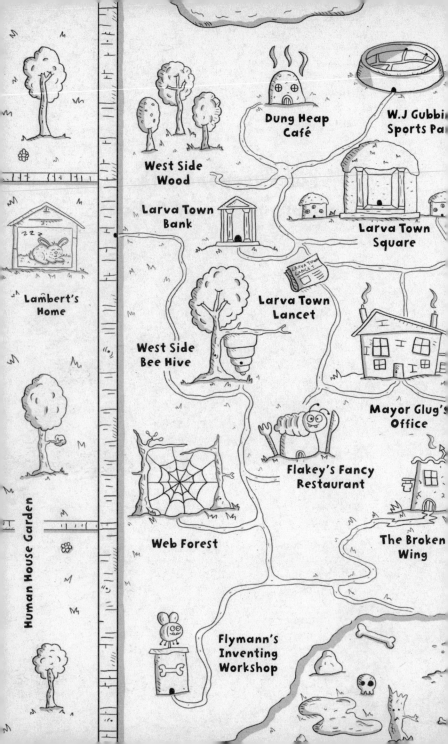

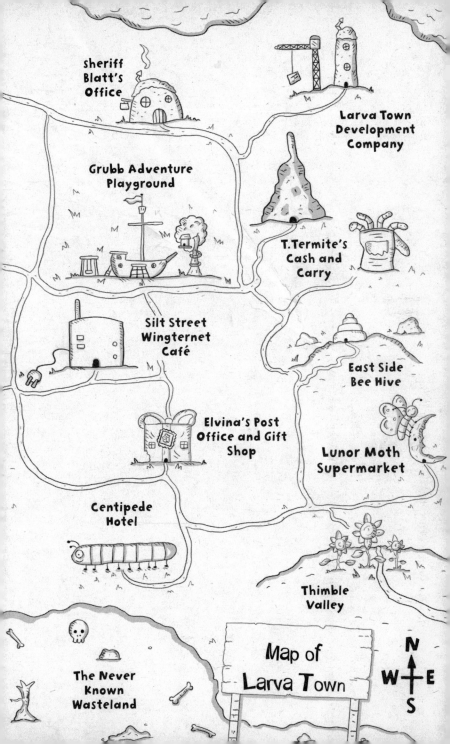

# CHAPTER 1

It was late afternoon in Larva Town. The
sky was a deep blue with tiny patches
of cloud and a light breeze was rustling
through the trees. Buzz and Itch, the
town's two crime-crushing Fleatectives,
were in a small glade. Buzz was sitting
on a rock reading the *Larva Town Lancet*.

Itch was taking photos of himself for their new glossy brochure. Nearby two young dung beetles were arguing over whose turn it was to play in a filthy pool of water while their grandfather was snoring loudly in a leaf hammock.

"Smile!" said Itch as he swung his camera over his head to take another shot of himself. But the camera hit him in the thorax and sent him flying backwards into a bush.

"*Fascinating*," murmured Buzz.

"You think my photos are going to be awesome?" asked Itch, scrambling out of the bush and gingerly stroking his thorax.

"No," replied Buzz, "it's this article in the paper."

Itch put down his camera and walked over to take a look at the *Lancet*.

# LARVA TOWN LANCET

The only newspaper you can eat

## GLOW-WORM THEFT AND HOUSE ROBBERIES ON SOUTH SIDE

Last night on the south side of town, the street-lighting glow-worm on Daffodil Place suddenly went out and vanished. A mayfly living on the street described the event in dramatic detail.

"Er, like, one second the street was lit up and, er, the next second it was kind of, like, all dark."

Moments after the glow-worm went down, a range of precious items were stolen from several insect dwellings, including a carpet moth's favourite carpet beater and a silkworm family's extra-silky bathing costumes.

The town's law enforcer, Sheriff Blatt, gave the following statement: "Whoever is behind  these glow-worm disappearances and house thefts had better look out because I'm on their case. That's after I've watched the first two episodes of *Earth Bug Crime Scene* and the series finale of *Water Boatmen Cops Undercover*."

Mayor Glug — when asked if he will be buying a new glow-worm for Daffodil Place — responded: "Although glow-worms don't need feeding, they charge a massive signing-on fee when they agree to work for me. As I haven't got enough money to buy any decent biscuits for my biscuit tin, I can't afford to replace this stolen one. So Daffodil Place will have to make do with other, inferior forms of lighting for the time being."

"What a clever ruse," murmured Buzz.

"Having a biscuit tin?" asked Itch.

"No," said Buzz, "the nature of this crime. First they grab the light and then they steal whatever they want in the darkness and mayhem. Looks like we're dealing with a very crafty mind."

"Not as crafty as *my* mind," said Itch, pointing to his brain with one of his legs.

"I say it's time for action!" announced Buzz, leaping to his feet.

"What . . . you want me to take a single photo of you and include it among

the hundreds of me in the brochure?"
asked Itch.

"No," replied Buzz. "We're going to
the South Side to investigate these crimes.
Sheriff Blatt may be glued to his flat-
screen TV, but real crime crushers have
no time for insect TV shows."

"Not even *Crickets Do the Craziest Things*?" asked Itch with disappointment.

"Absolutely not!" cried Buzz. "And since Daffodil Place will be pretty dark by the time we get there, these might come in handy." He grabbed two twigs off the ground.

"Are you going to use those to beat off any attackers?" asked Itch.

Buzz sighed and started walking.

On their walk to the South Side, Buzz and Itch played Insect I-Spy. The game didn't last long, though, because Itch kept saying that he spied something beginning with the letter "I", which always turned out to be himself. When Buzz pointed out that this made the game a little bit boring, Itch started sulking and only cheered up when Buzz said *he* spotted something beginning with the letter "I", which turned out to be . . . Itch.

By the time they reached Daffodil Place the sun had nearly set, and with no glow-worm to light up the street, the residents had placed small beeswax candles on the ground at regular intervals. These gave off an eerie glow.

"OK," nodded Buzz. "Let's start with some door-to-door enquiries."

The first dwelling they approached was a tall mud hut. They knocked on the door. It opened on a chain.

"Yes?" asked a frowning, elderly stick insect.

"It's about the glow-worm burglary and the thefts that followed last night," said Buzz. "My crime-crushing partner and I are trying to track down the culprits."

"It wasn't *me!*" replied the stick insect.

"We're not saying it was you,"
responded Buzz.

"Aren't we?" asked Itch.

"No," grimaced Buzz, "we just want to
know if you saw or heard anything."

"I didn't see or hear *me* committing

any crimes," snapped the stick insect.

"We understand," said Buzz, "it's just that. . ."

But Buzz didn't get to finish his sentence. That was because a distant rumbling sound could be heard nearby, followed shortly by a series of loud shrieks.

"QUICK!" shouted Buzz, speeding off in the direction of the noise. Itch gave the stick insect a suspicious glance and raced after Buzz. They ran to the end of Daffodil Place and swerved round the corner on to Yellow Seed Avenue, where they stopped dead in their tracks.

The whole street had been plunged into darkness.

The glow-worm grabbers had struck again.

# Can you find the missing words?

Z J G X A Y I R F S U E
S P D R S J H U S T M L
T J E Q A A G E T J U R
H M S F D B N B S P D T
G F T D S K B A W Y Z Z
I Y R G R T U E O W C O
L C J A V G Z V R Q U P
O A D L C F Z T M S G H
F G D I N C A K B C F O
T Y E T M L G L O W E D
A L A C N J B S C B Z L
M R V H V Y S T E A L M

BUZZ
ITCH
GLOW
WORM

STEAL
DARKNESS
GRABBERS
LIGHTS

Answers at the back of the book

# CHAPTER 2

In the darkness the Fleatectives could just
about make out a series of insects who
were screaming and howling.

"My triple-decker wood sandwich was
snatched when the glow-worm light went
out," wept a distraught termite.

"All of my Beetles records have been
stolen!" despaired a heartbroken slug.

"My sunflower smoothie maker has
gone!" cried a devastated tapeworm.

"Can someone please provide us with a
bit of light?" said Buzz.

The termite who'd had her wood

sandwich stolen stopped weeping for a moment and lit a beeswax candle. Buzz marched over to her and dipped the two twigs he'd brought with him into the candle's flame. Instantly they were transformed into flaming torches. He held one above his head and handed the other to Itch.

All of the insects on Yellow Seed Avenue suddenly went quiet and turned to face the Fleatectives.

"We understand how terrible this must be for all of you," announced Buzz, his face illuminated by the torch's glow, "but we're going to catch whoever did this and get back all of your stolen items."

"Maybe not *all*," cut in Itch. "I mean, if I was hungry after a robbery, I'd probably eat the wood sandwich on the way back to my crime lair."

The termite gulped in distress and Buzz gave Itch a hard shove in the abdomen.

"Did anyone see or hear anything suspicious before the light went out?" Buzz asked the frightened residents.

"I saw something after the light went out," said the slug who'd had her Beetles records stolen.

"Was it a film?" asked Itch. "I'm always looking for good recommendations."

Buzz shook his head despairingly.

"I saw two suspicious-looking figures scuttling off down the street carrying bags over their shoulders," said the slug. "It looked like a butterfly and a woodlouse."

"Moth-erama!" cried Itch. "That sounds like The Painted Lady and Crustman!"

The Painted Lady – a sinister butterfly – and her beefy woodlouse sidekick, Crustman, were suspected of carrying out a vast range of crimes in Larva Town, but no crime crusher or law enforcer had ever managed to nail them.

"Would you be prepared to stand up in insect court and repeat what you've just said?" asked Buzz.

The slug nodded.

"Then my crime-crushing partner and I will immediately go and share this information with Sheriff Blatt," announced Buzz.

"Do we have to?" moaned Itch. "If we tell Blatt, he'll claim all the credit for himself, while we do all of the legwork!"

"Don't worry about who gets the credit," chided Buzz. "Let's stop those glow-worm-snatching villains first!"

There were cheers from the insects on Yellow Seed Avenue.

"But before we go," said Buzz, "I think we should take a quick look at where the glow-worm was stationed."

Holding their fire torches in front of them, the Fleatectives climbed up the side of the slug's hut. In the middle of some criss-crossed wires (that were attached to buildings on either side of the street) was a tree trunk. This was topped with soft grass to give the glow-worm a comfortable resting place.

"I can't see anything apart from a few strands of coloured material," said Buzz, holding his torch up as the Fleatectives stepped on to the trunk.

"I bet they're from The Painted Lady and Crustman's swag bags," replied Itch.

"You may well be right," nodded Buzz. "We need to find the sheriff."

Fifteen minutes later Itch was pressing
his face up to the window at the front
of Sheriff Blatt's office, saying, "I can't see
him."

"Let's try round the back," said Buzz.
"That's where his TV room is."

But the giant TV screen was off and
there was no sign of the cockroach sheriff
anywhere. Buzz and Itch had just come
back to the front of the office when a
high-pitched voice called out to them.

"If you're looking for the sheriff, he'll be at the Centipede Hotel," said an ant who was sweeping the road. "He's there tonight for a card game."

On hearing this news, Itch immediately began shaking his body from side to side and going very red in the face.

"What are you doing?" demanded Buzz.

"I'm trying to fly!" gasped Itch. "It would be much quicker to get to the Centipede Hotel by air."

"We're *fleas*, Itch," said Buzz. "We jump; we don't fly!"

Itch sighed with disappointment and reluctantly stopped shaking.

The Centipede Hotel was at the end of a narrow cul-de-sac. It was made out of dried mud, twigs and flattened pebbles, and bore a large neon sign stating:

# THE CENTIPEDE HOTEL & LOUNGE BAR

## A HUNDRED DIFFERENT ROOMS AT A HUNDRED DIFFERENT PRICES.

The reception area was a long narrow room with a bamboo desk in the middle. On top of the desk was a metal bath filled to the brim with wet soil. A centipede was inside the bath; the only visible part of him was his green and yellow head.

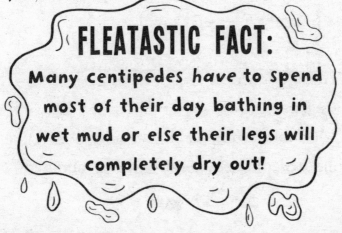

**FLEATASTIC FACT:**
Many centipedes have to spend most of their day bathing in wet mud or else their legs will completely dry out!

"Good evening," said the centipede in a smooth tone, "the name's Jester. I'm the proprietor, chef, bottle washer and insect bouncer for this establishment. How can I help you?"

"I'd like to know if you have a hundred different rooms with a hundred different prices because you have a hundred different legs?" asked Itch.

"We centipedes don't usually have a hundred legs," replied Jester. "In fact, I've got a mere forty-six. I have a hundred rooms because I like the number."

"I prefer the number ninety-nine," said Itch.

"How can I help you?" asked Jester.

"We're looking for Sheriff Blatt," said Itch.

"And you are?"

Buzz held out his Fleatectives business card.

Jester nodded and turned slightly in the soil. "You'll find him in the Mulch Lounge," he replied, "third floor."

Fleatectives crime CRUSHING Agency

Find Itch and Buzz on Lambert the Rabbit

Buzz and Itch climbed the wobbly wooden stairs to the third floor and reached a white door marked:

## MULCH LOUNGE

Buzz knocked with his antennae.

"Enter!" called the sheriff's deep voice.

Buzz pushed the door open and the Fleatectives stepped inside. The Mulch Lounge was square shaped and dimly lit. The walls were covered in old paintings of centipede knights carrying out a series of heroic acts, like holding a sword with every leg, or clinging on to a speeding horse's tail and using their legs to fire multiple arrows from multiple bows.

But Buzz and Itch's attention was immediately drawn to the circular brick table in the centre of the room. On it stood a collection of aphid-juice bottles, drinking thimbles and packets of earwax nuts. Sitting at the table were three characters, reclining on nettle chairs and holding insect playing cards close to their chests. These characters were Sheriff Blatt . . . The Painted Lady and Crustman.

The sheriff was a brown cockroach with a white "S" on his crusty back. The Painted Lady was a butterfly with exquisite orange, white and black patterns on her wings. Crustman was a woodlouse who had a gormless stare and eyes that shone with the possibility of violence.

"Sheriff Blatt!" exclaimed Buzz in surprise. "It is not up to me to choose the company you keep, but I can assure you that the two creatures you are currently playing cards with are nothing but despicable criminals."

"Yeah!" nodded Itch. "They just carried out a glow-worm snatch and several house robberies on Yellow Seed Avenue."

"And we reckon they were behind the exact same crime on Daffodil Place last night," said Buzz.

"They must have just got here," added Itch. "I bet the glow-worm and that stolen gear aren't very far away."

"And what proof have you got that my two card-playing associates have anything to do with these crimes?" demanded Sheriff Blatt haughtily.

"We have a slug witness who saw a dodgy-looking butterfly and woodlouse – exactly matching these two's appearance – running away with swag bags moments after the crime tonight!" said Itch triumphantly.

The Painted Lady let out a high-pitched

laugh and Crustman chuckled in a horrible low tone.

"I think you'll find that these crimes are no laughing matter," tutted Itch.

"And I think *you'll* find that your slug friend is mistaken," sneered The Painted Lady.

"Sorry, amateurs, but these two have absolutely nothing to do with any glow-worm theft or stealing spree," said Sheriff Blatt firmly.

"And how on insect earth can you know that?" demanded Itch.

"Because I was here with them at the exact time the Daffodil Place crimes occurred last night," replied the sheriff, "and I've been holed up playing cards with them here tonight, for the last TWO HOURS."

# Can you spot the eight differences between these two images?

Answers at the back of the book

# CHAPTER 3

"TWO HOURS!" blurted out Itch.

"Two hours!" nodded Blatt, pouring some aphid juice into one of the empty thimbles and taking a long gulp.

"Oh dear," said The Painted Lady with a cruel twist in her voice, "I think you've got your facts ever so slightly WRONG!"

"Hang on a minute, Sheriff Blatt!" blurted out Buzz. "Our streets are being plunged into darkness, insects' precious items are being stolen, and all you can do is sit in this lounge playing cards with these two suspects! Shouldn't you be out there trying to crack the case?"

"I don't need to be *out there*," replied the sheriff. "I can solve the case perfectly well from here."

"But you haven't even visited the crime scenes!" pointed out Itch.

"I can reconstruct the crime scenes in my mind," replied Blatt.

Crustman cracked his shell and gave the Fleatectives a hateful glare.

"Why don't you two just run along and leave the crime-solving to the professionals," said the sheriff, chucking a leg-full of earwax nuts into his mouth.

"M – m-maybe they put sleeping potion in your aphid juice," spluttered Itch, "and then while you were asleep they sneaked out, nicked the glow-worm and the other stuff, and then raced back here before you woke up!"

"I think I'd know if I'd been asleep,"

replied the sheriff.

"Aha!" cried Itch. "I think I know where
the stolen glow-worms, the other booty
and your swag bags are being hidden!" He
stepped over to a loose piece of wallpaper
and gave it a hard tug with his mouth-
parts. A huge area of wallpaper peeled away,
revealing . . . an empty area of wall.

"I think it's time you left before you do any further damage," snapped The Painted Lady in a menacing tone.

"We're leaving," muttered Buzz, crossing back to the door while peering round the room in a last attempt to spot the stolen goods.

"And anyway," said Itch, joining his partner, "just because you have a completely watertight alibi doesn't mean you're innocent."

"Get lost!" snarled Crustman. "Or I'll grip you and grasp you and grill you!"

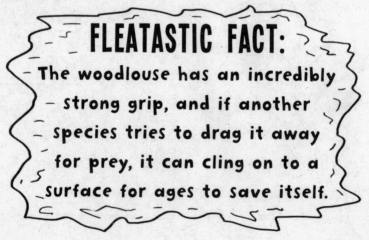

**FLEATASTIC FACT:** The woodlouse has an incredibly strong grip, and if another species tries to drag it away for prey, it can cling on to a surface for ages to save itself.

The Fleatectives – feeling hot and humiliated – traipsed back downstairs, bid farewell to Jester and his mud bath, and found themselves back in the street.

"Do you think the sheriff is telling the truth?" mused Itch. "Maybe he's covering for The Painted Lady and Crustman in return for receiving a share of their criminal profits?"

"Sheriff Blatt may be a lazy, self-loving, TV-obsessed, smarmy creep, but he's no crook," said Buzz.

"So if the slug *is* telling the truth about what she saw, what does it mean?" enquired Itch.

"It means that either The Painted Lady and Crustman have got some ingenious way of being in two places at the same time, or there's another butterfly and woodlouse crime team," replied Buzz.

"I'd love to be in two places at the same time," said Itch, running madly from one patch of ground to another in an attempt to achieve this feat.

"Forget it," sighed Buzz. "Let's head home and see what we can find."

Home was a female rabbit called Lambert. She lived in a small hutch at the bottom of a human family's garden. Lambert had luxurious soft white fur, pale pink eyes and sticking-up ears. She spent most of her time snoozing, something which baffled Buzz and Itch because she hardly ever did anything that could possibly make her tired. She was fast asleep when they reached her.

The Fleatectives gave her a quick bite each.

"Ow!" winced Lambert, opening one eye. "How many times have I told you not to bite me?"

"And how many times have we told you that we only do it when we're hungry?" responded Buzz.

Lambert closed her eye.

"There was another glow-worm theft followed by house robberies tonight," Buzz announced.

"We have a slug witness who saw a butterfly and a woodlouse at the scene," said Itch.

"The Painted Lady and Crustman?" asked Lambert, opening one eye again.

"We thought so," replied Buzz, "but Sheriff Blatt insists they were with him at the time when both crimes took place."

"And when we paid them a visit there was no sign of the stolen glow-worms or the snatched items," added Itch.

"Can you think of any other butterfly and woodlouse crime team?" asked Buzz.

Lambert stretched. "I don't know of one, but I *have* heard there's a place out of town where stolen goods are bought and sold. If The Painted Lady and Crustman are behind these crimes, that's where they might sell the glow-worms and the other stolen things."

"Really?" asked Buzz. "Where is it?"

"It's just beyond the Never Known Wasteland," replied Lambert.

Buzz's eyes opened wide.

Itch gulped and hid behind Buzz.

The Never Known Wasteland was a place that people only talked about in whispers.

"Who owns this stolen goods place?" asked Buzz.

"It's run by a spider called Alfie Rocks," yawned Lambert. "A dodgier arachnid is apparently hard to find."

"Thanks for the tip, Lambert," shuddered Itch, sticking his head out from behind Buzz's back, "but obviously we won't be visiting there."

"On the contrary," said Buzz firmly. "That's exactly where we're going first thing in the morning!"

# Help Buzz and Itch find their way to the Never Known Wasteland

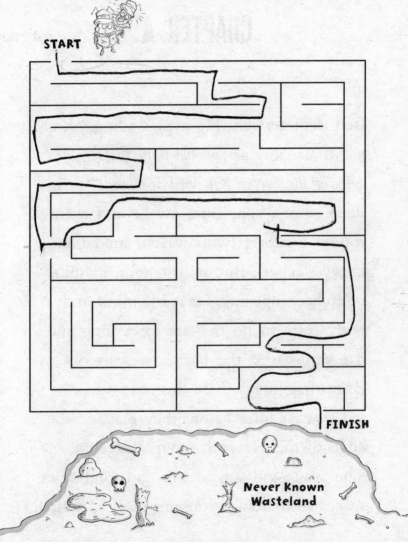

START

FINISH

Never Known Wasteland

**Answers at the back of the book**

# CHAPTER 4

Itch slept terribly. He kept wailing, "*Keep me as far away as possible from the terrible evils of the Never Known Wasteland!*" in his sleep, which kept Buzz awake and even roused Lambert (who was an incredibly heavy sleeper). But at first light, in spite of Itch complaining that his mind and body were in no fit state for a long and dangerous trek, the Fleatectives set out, Buzz dragging Itch by his antennae.

It wasn't long before they reached the edge of the Never Known Wasteland. The Wasteland was a dark and foreboding space, with strange-looking bushes, twisted trunks of dead trees and bones scattered on the floor. A brown mist swirled inside it. Itch fell dramatically on to the floor, clutched his thorax and croaked, "I'm dying!"

"Crime crushers don't die that easily," scolded ~~Itch~~, dragging ~~Buzz~~ to his feet
and steering him on to the path that led round the perimeter of the Wasteland. After twenty-five minutes and a lot of moaning from Itch they reached the end of the Wasteland and emerged into a large muddy field. At the far end was some sort of two-storey wooden shack.

As they got closer they saw a line of insects queuing in front of a door that was splintered and peeling. Stuck at a sloping angle on a second-floor window was a sign declaring:

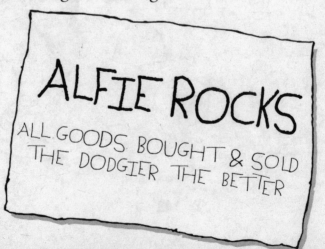

"Remember," whispered Buzz, as they neared the shack, "we're not Fleatectives."

"Of course we are!" replied Itch. "It says so on our business cards."

"No!" hissed Buzz. "I mean, for the purposes of the other customers and for Alfie Rocks. If any of them find out we're crime crushers, they'll crush *us*."

"Oh, I get it," nodded Itch, frowning and curling his lip to try and look as un-Fleatective-like as possible.

They joined the queue.

An earwig in front of them was holding a battered automatic fur-brusher and tapping his forcep pincers nervously on his abdomen. A moth in front of the earwig was cradling a broken nettle-slicer with a sticker in another language on its packaging. A family of termites in front of the moth were empty-handed and discussing what sort of dodgy bark-soufflé maker they should buy.

"How much do you think I'll get for this?" asked the earwig anxiously as he chewed on something mouldy and foul-smelling. He turned to face Buzz and Itch while nodding at the damaged fur-brusher.

"It fell off the back of an insect lorry."

"Well why didn't you hand it back to the insect lorry driver?" asked Itch.

Buzz kicked one of Itch's claws and said, "It looks in great shape. I reckon you'll get a good price."

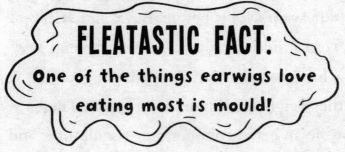

**FLEATASTIC FACT:**
One of the things earwigs love eating most is mould!

"*How much of this gear do you think is stolen?*" whispered Itch, when the earwig had turned away again.

"*Most of it*," muttered Buzz, "*but it would probably be hard to prove it.*"

The queue was moving pretty quickly and insects kept emerging from the interior – a yellow dung fly came out struggling under the weight of an all-in-one insect exercise machine with several missing parts, and a wood ant stepped out looking angry to only have a tiny stack of Bug notes strapped to his back.

"Looks like Alfie drives a hard bargain," whispered Buzz.

It wasn't long before Buzz and Itch were inside the shack. At the far end was a long wooden counter groaning under the weight of hundreds of items. There were insect earphones, grass sculptures and sunflower banjos – all in bad shape – to name but a few. A huge hairy tarantula with a goatee beard was examining goods on the counter, taking in loads of Bug notes, handing out far less and continually shouting, "ME LOVE MONEY! ME WANT MORE!"

Just looking at Alfie Rocks made Itch's whole body quiver with fear.

"Keep your eyes peeled for The Painted Lady and Crustman and for any of the goods that were stolen at Yellow Seed Avenue and Daffodil Place," whispered Buzz.

Itch strained his neck to look at the counter, but he couldn't see the suspects or any wood sandwiches, extra-silky bathing costumes or Beetles records.

As they moved forward, Buzz spotted a flight of half-hidden wooden steps to their right.

"If we can't find anything down here," said Buzz, "we need to look upstairs."

"Nice idea," nodded Itch. "I'll just ask Mr Rocks if he's OK with that."

Buzz clamped a leg over Itch's mouth and hissed, "Don't be crazy! Just follow me."

As Alfie Rocks demonstrated a smashed-up insect toy kitchen with detachable dung chute to a fungus gnat, the Fleatectives silently peeled away from the queue. The giraffe weevil who was behind them gave them a suspicious look, but Buzz shot him a confident smile that said, *What we are about to do is completely reasonable and normal so please don't raise the alarm!*

The first stair creaked, as did the second and third, and Buzz and Itch worried that this sound would attract the attention of Alfie Rocks. But he was too busy taking a large wad of Bug notes from the fungus gnat and crowing, "ME LOVE MONEY! ME WANT MORE!"

Buzz and Itch hurried up the rest of the stairs. At the top were three doors leading off from a narrow landing. Buzz gently nudged open the one directly in front of them. It was empty except for

two large bags on the floor. Buzz had a
rummage inside but found nothing apart
from dressing-up clothes – lots of insect
costumes and headgear.

"Look at me, I'm The Painted Lady,"
laughed Itch. "This must be a spider kid's
room."

They moved on to the room next door.
This contained a bed and three large
floor-to-ceiling cupboards. Buzz and Itch
opened them and found masses of spider

memorabilia: spider sports star collectors' cards, old-fashioned eight-legged fashion accessories, and posters of great spider actors and comedians from yesteryear.

The third room looked much more promising. This contained a mass of rusty iron trunks containing thousands of half-broken and wonky items, from mayfly mantelpiece ornaments to locust recipe books to guides on midge etiquette. But even though they searched very methodically, the Fleatectives didn't catch sign of anything they were looking for.

"This is Frustrating with a capital C," groaned Itch.

Buzz was just about to point out that "Frustrating" begins with a capital "F" when both Fleatectives were suddenly and violently hit on the back of their exoskeletons.

# Can you solve these word jumbles?

**1. CREAKS FOIL**

Alfie Rock

**2. CHAT ZZ IN BUD**

Itch and Buzz

**3. UNSET BOG**

bug notes

**4. A LAVENDER NEWTS KNOWN**

never known wasteland

**5. CEASE VET LIFT**

Heatectives

**Answers at the back of the book**

# CHAPTER 5

THWACK! Buzz and Itch smacked into a
wall and crashed down on to the ground.

"OW!" yelled Itch.

"OOF!" shouted Buzz.

They turned round and came face to
face with their attacker.

It was an elderly female spider with

fuzzy white hair

strands, incredibly

long legs and

blazing red

eyes. She

was wearing

a faded

blue baseball cap bearing the name of a company called World Wide Webbing and she was holding a large branch.

## FLEATASTIC FACT:

Some spiders have extremely long legs. The giant huntsman spider has a leg span of around thirty centimetres — that's as long as a ruler!

*SLAM!* She lashed out with the branch again, this time hitting the Fleatectives in their abdomens, which sent them crunching back against the wall.

"HANG ON A SECOND!" groaned Itch. "This isn't a fair fight. At least let us have a twig each!"

The spider let out a roar and aimed

her branch again.

But this time she didn't strike out. Instead she spoke – in a horrible wheezy voice.

"What do you think you two are doing, snooping around the upstairs of my boy's goods shack?" she demanded furiously. Her voice sounded as if she'd just swallowed a bucket of dry ice.

Buzz frowned at the strange wheezy way she spoke.

"Do I take it that you're Alfie Rocks' mother?" asked Itch. He and Buzz tried to stand up but she pinned them back to the floor with her branch.

"That's right!" she declared. "I'm Old Ma Rocks, mother of the most beautiful son in the world."

"When you say *beautiful*, do you mean *repulsively ugly*?" enquired Itch.

Buzz shot him a fierce look.

"I asked you what you're doing up here," snarled Old Ma Rocks suspiciously, letting out a few more wheezes. "Are you detectives or law people or something like that?"

"No way!" cried Itch. "At least, not while we're inside your son's disreputable business establishment."

"Of course we aren't detectives or law people!" insisted Buzz. "We're *collectors*. We thought the upstairs was part of this wonderful store."

"Yeah," nodded Itch energetically. "We're BIG collectors. We collect grumpy old spider mothers like you."

"HOW DARE YOU!" roared Old Ma Rocks, her eyes huge circles of flaming fury as she raised the branch above her head.

"No, no, no!" cut in Buzz quickly. "What my friend means is we collect *funky old spider memorabilia* – you know, things like spider sports star collectors' cards, old-fashioned eight-legged fashion accessories, and posters of great spider actors and comedians from yesteryear."

"Well, why didn't you say so?" wheezed Old Ma Rocks, throwing her branch on to the floor and helping the Fleatectives up with her legs. "Alfie has tons of that stuff in the room next door. I'll just go down and take over from him at the till so he can come up and personally show it all to you."

"You don't need to do that," responded Buzz quickly.

"Don't be silly!" wheezed Old Ma Rocks. "He knows the collection far better than I do. And besides, he loves money, and I'm sure he'll persuade you to spend LOADS of it here!"

"PLEASE DON'T GET HIM!" begged Itch, imagining Alfie Rocks' legs curling round his thorax when he realized the Fleatectives weren't really collectors and had absolutely no intention of spending any money in the store.

"We accept Bug notes and Leg-it cards," said Old Ma Rocks.

"We'd love to spend loads of money here," said Buzz, "but unfortunately we left our flea wallets at home."

"What kind of collectors leave home without their wallets?" frowned Old Ma Rocks suspiciously.

"Foolish ones," replied Buzz.

"Ones with bad memories," added Itch helpfully.

Old Ma Rocks wheezed again and looked towards her branch.

"Don't hit us again," pleaded Itch. "It's been proved by insect doctors that hitting fleas isn't good for their health."

"Fine," snarled Old Ma Rocks with a loud wheeze, "but make sure you do come back with those wallets. If you don't, Alfie and I will come and find you and mash you into flea paste. You got that?"

"A hundred per cent," nodded Buzz, grabbing one of his partner's claws and backing both Fleatectives towards the door.

They shot downstairs, barged past the queue and raced out into the sunlight, almost knocking over the family of termites who were now the proud owners of a half-split-open bark-soufflé maker.

They
sprinted
across the
field and
jumped on
to the path
leading
round the
perimeter of the
Never Known Wasteland and didn't stop
running until they'd reached the other
end.

"Well, that was a complete waste of
time," panted Itch.

"I'm not sure it was a *complete* waste,"
replied Buzz. "If anyone is going to handle
the stolen glow-worms and the other
nicked stuff, I reckon it'll be the Rocks."

"But we didn't see ANY of the
stuff from Daffodil Place or Yellow

Seed Avenue," pointed out Itch, "and The Painted Lady and Crustman were definitely not there."

"True," nodded Buzz, "but I still say we keep an eye on Alfie and his mum."

"Well, let's do it from a very great distance and in full camouflage gear," shuddered Itch, "because being mashed into flea paste isn't one of my top priorities at the moment."

Buzz nodded thoughtfully. Being mashed into flea paste wasn't one of his top priorities either.

"I have a message for you," announced a very sleepy Lambert when Buzz and Itch got home.

"It's not from Alfie or Old Ma Rocks, is it?" asked Itch anxiously.

"No," yawned Lambert. "It's from Mayor Glug. He wants you to go to his office straight away."

"Haven't we got time for a quick drink?" asked Itch, eyeing Lambert's skin hungrily.

"No," replied Lambert quickly, "he said it was urgent."

Mayor Glug's office was in the centre of Larva Town. It was made of blue stones and finely cut wooden joists. On the first floor were rooms for the mayor's staff. The second floor was his space. It was a huge open room encircled by glass so that the mayor had a three-hundred-and-sixty-degree view of the town. To the left was his desk – a huge oak rectangle. At the far end were three plush soft grass sofas. When Buzz and Itch showed up, Mayor Glug was standing while Sheriff Blatt sitting on one of the sofas.

Mayor Glug was a mantis with a long thin flat back, a triangular face and piercing green eyes.

"Glad you could make it, boys," called the mayor, waving them over.

Buzz and Itch sat down on a sofa each.

"Greetings, failed amateur sleuths," grinned the sheriff.

"Can I get you anything to eat or drink?" enquired the mayor.

"Let me see," said Itch. "Could I have some wood strip fries, a double portion of soil pancakes and a large glass of nettle juice?"

"We're fine," said Buzz, frowning at Itch. "What can we do for you, Mayor?"

"It's about these glow-worm thefts," said the mayor. "I've already lost two, and as I'm sure you know, I won't be replacing them because. . ."

". . .you haven't even got enough money to buy any decent biscuits for your biscuit tin," said Itch, finishing his sentence.

The mayor nodded at Itch.

"Mayor Glug," said Sheriff Blatt smoothly, "you don't need to worry about this situation and you certainly don't need to involve these two boys. I'll be able to wrap up the case very soon. It'll just have to wait until I've watched my box set of *Epic Ladybird Detective Car Chases*."

"You won't be able to wrap anything up," snapped Itch, "because you're doing NOTHING!"

"I'll wrap you up in a minute!" shot back Blatt.

"I'll snap you up!" growled Itch.

"I'll zap you up!"

"I'll flap you up!"

"I'll bap you up!"

"I'll nap you up!"

"I'll—"

"THAT'S ENOUGH!" shouted Buzz. "Let's hear what the mayor has to say!"

"What I'm saying," said Mayor Glug, as Itch and Blatt glared at each other, "is that if this continues, I'll be forced to take down ALL of the town's glow-worms. I simply can't afford to lose any more."

"But if you take down every glow-worm and all we have is beeswax candles, the robbers will have won!" cried Buzz in horror. "There'll be enough darkness for them and any other villains to steal whatever they want in any part of town!"

"It will be total chaos!" nodded Itch. "Everyone will be terrified. Insects will probably start moving away. Come on, Mayor Glug – it could spell THE END for Larva Town!" Said Itch.

"I'm sorry," sighed the mayor heavily, "but if one more glow-worm is stolen, it's lights out for ALL the others."

# Which Mayor Glug is the odd one out?

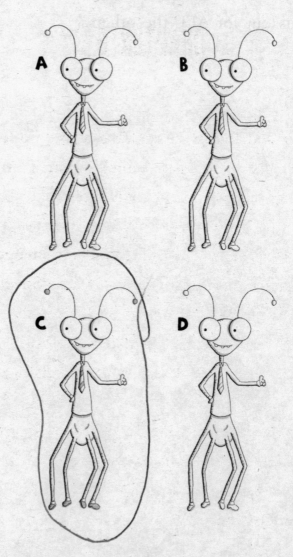

Answers at the back of the book

# CHAPTER 6

Buzz and Itch were standing at the bottom of a very high bamboo building on Corn Street. It was several hours after their meeting at the mayor's office and they'd both had a nap to build up their strength for the evening's adventures. Corn Street was connected to Yellow Seed Avenue. Buzz was convinced that if the glow-worm thieves were going to strike again, this was where they'd choose. It seemed that they were making their thieving way through Larva Town road-by-road.

"Let's go," said Buzz. "We've got a sizeable climb."

The bamboo building was home to sixteen different families of mayflies. It was getting late and as Buzz and Itch climbed, they saw several sets of mayfly parents yelling at their children to brush their wings and go to bed. When they reached the roof, the Fleatectives lay on their fronts and looked out on to Corn Street.

A short way down the road stood a tree trunk, from where a series of criss-crossed wires were attached to several building fronts. On top of the trunk sat a plump glow-worm. A few minutes later as the sun dipped beyond the horizon, two segments at the end of the glow-worm's body and two small dots on the underside of her tail lit up in a yellowy green light, bathing Corn Street with a warm glow.

"I wish *I* could light up," murmured Itch, lifting the back of his body in an

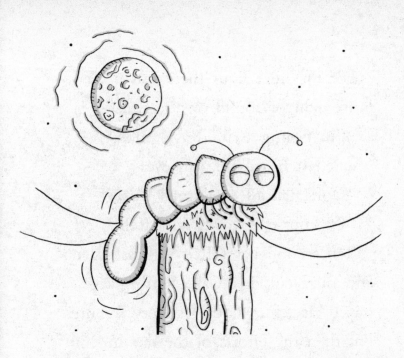

attempt to squeeze some light out of it.

Buzz shook his head in despair and continued watching the street.

For an hour there was a lot of activity on Corn Street. Some fruit flies got back from a party and crashed noisily into their flat while a group of gnat teenagers nattered on the kerb. All the while the glow-worm kept up her bright glow and the Fleatectives watched.

For the next hour there was no movement or sound on the street.

"I'm feeling as tired as Lambert," yawned Itch, rubbing his eyes.

"Don't fall asleep," urged Buzz.

"Of course I won't," said Itch.

Ten seconds later Itch was fast asleep and Buzz couldn't wake him. Buzz stayed alert for another twenty minutes, but then the efforts of the day hit him hard, and very soon he too fell into a deep sleep.

Buzz and Itch were jolted awake by a blood-curdling scream.

"MY COLLECTION OF RARE DUNGHILL MAPS HAS BEEN STOLEN!"

Buzz leapt to his feet; Itch struggled to his.

Corn Street was dark. The glow-worm had gone. The robberies had started.

"QUICK!" yelled Buzz, racing back down the building as fast as his flea legs could carry him.

"WAIT FOR ME!" shouted Itch, legging it after him.

"MY ONION SEED TAPESTRY HAS VANISHED!" yelled a voice below.

"LOOK!" cried Itch as the Fleatectives zoomed downwards.

At the far end of Corn Street – which was illuminated by light from the next street, Breeze Crescent – Buzz and Itch saw two shadows rushing across the front of some buildings.

They were unmistakably the shadows of a butterfly and a woodlouse.

A distant noise was coming from the same direction.

"So the thieves *are* The Painted Lady and Crustman!" gasped Itch. "They must have somehow tricked Sheriff Blatt into giving them an alibi for the other two thefts!"

"Well, we won't let him give them one tonight!" said Buzz as they hit the pavement.

"What are we going to do?" asked Itch.

"The Painted Lady can fly, so she's a lot faster than us," said Buzz, "but Crustman is slower."

"I hardly think this is the time to be organizing an insect Olympics," tutted Itch.

**FLEATASTIC FACT:**
Painted Lady butterflies can fly up to speeds of thirty miles per hour and can cover distances of one hundred miles in a single day.

"No!" groaned Buzz. "What I'm saying is that they always travel *together* and Crustman will slow them down. So if we rush straight to the Centipede Hotel, we'll arrive first and find Sheriff Blatt alone and we'll be there when The Painted Lady and Crustman show up with their swag bags!

That way the sheriff won't be able to give them an alibi and we can close the case!"

"But Blatt will say he solved the crime," said Itch sourly.

"He can say what he wants, Itch. Now come on!"

Buzz and Itch made it to the Centipede Hotel in record time, raced through reception (where they shouted a brief hello to Jester, who was rotating in his metal mud bath), ran up the stairs and burst into the Mulch Lounge.

The sight that greeted their eyes made their entire bodies freeze. For there in front of them sat Sheriff Blatt with . . . The Painted Lady and Crustman.

Each of them was holding playing cards, each of them was looking relaxed, and none of them looked like they'd just sprinted there from a crime scene.

"AAAAARRRRRGGGGHHHHH!" screamed Itch.

"IT'S NOT POSSIBLE!" shouted Buzz. "WE JUST SAW YOU RUNNING AWAY FROM CORN STREET AFTER ANOTHER GLOW-WORM THEFT!"

"YOU MUST HAVE A TWIN BROTHER AND A TWIN SISTER!" cried Itch.

"We're both only children," sneered The Painted Lady as Crustman stood up and towered menacingly over the Fleatectives.

"They've been here for well over an hour," said Sheriff Blatt. "They can't have been at Corn Street."

"Can you time travel?" asked Itch in desperation. "Is that it? Or shape shift or split your bodies in two in some gruesome magical feat?"

"I've told you two all along to leave the case cracking to the town's only proper law enforcer," said Sheriff Blatt, shaking his head sadly. He took a sip of aphid juice and coughed loudly.

A look of wonder suddenly passed across Buzz's face. "That's it," he said, "I've got it!"

"You've worked out how The Painted Lady and Crustman can be in two places at the same time?" asked Itch.

"No!" declared Buzz, darting away from Crustman. "They're not the thieves!"

"W . . . w . . . what are you talking about?" demanded Itch in total confusion, "W . . . w . . . where are you going?"

"To the Never Known Wasteland!" declared Buzz, racing out of the door.

# Can you fill in
# the missing letters?

1. B_U_ZZ

2. I_R_ _S_H

3. _T_HE _P_A_I_NTED _L_AD_Y_

4. C_R_US_T_M_ _N_

5. _S_HE_R_I_FF B_I_ _S_TT

6. F_L_EA_T_ _A_CTIV_E_S

Answers at the back of the book

# CHAPTER 7

"Are you out of your tiny insect mind?" screamed Itch, racing after Buzz down the wooden stairs and past Jester into the cool night air. "We skirted round the Never Known Wasteland in the day and that was bad enough, but at night it will be a million times more scary! And anyway, why are we going there? Is it connected to some kind of special powers that The Painted Lady and Crustman have?"

But Buzz didn't answer any of these questions. He was too busy running.

Itch was right – the Never Known

Wasteland *did* look a million times more scary at night, and several times he tried to jump on Buzz's back (without succeeding).

When they reached the far side of the Wasteland, Buzz made a beeline for Alfie Rocks' shack.

"What in flying ant's name are you doing?" exclaimed Itch. "Remember what Old Ma Rocks said she'd do to us if we came back here *without* loads of cash?"

But Buzz sprinted towards the shack.

"We checked it out earlier," protested Itch, trying to pull Buzz back. Buzz pushed him off and started walking round the shack. The front was all locked up and the building was completely quiet.

"They must store the stolen stuff somewhere," muttered Buzz to himself.

"We looked downstairs, we looked

upstairs, we looked into Old Ma Rock's terrifying eyes and we realized this wasn't a place for a couple of fleas like us!" whined Itch.

"Where is it?" tutted Buzz, walking round to the back of the building. He stepped past a large empty wheelbarrow and peered through a window.

Itch (wanting to be as far away from the shack as possible, in case Alfie Rocks or his fearsome mother burst outside) wandered over to a clump of trees and started shaking his abdomen from side to side and stamping his legs on the ground. Faster and faster his body moved, and soon it was a blur.

"What are you doing?" hissed Buzz, walking over and grabbing Itch's body to make him stop.

"I'm trying to fly away from this place," replied Itch. "I think I was nearly there."

"You don't fly. You can't fly. You won't fly. You SHAN'T FLY, Itch, and that's because you're a FLEA!!!" said Buzz. "We don't fly, we jump!"

Itch sighed sadly, but to cheer himself up he jumped as high into the air as he could (which felt a tiny bit like flying). He landed on the side of a tree trunk and jumped several more times until he reached the top. As he did this, one of his legs hit something smooth and square, and a second later there was a whirring sound. To Itch's astonishment a wooden circle started moving aside until there was a circular opening at the top of the trunk.

"I think you should see this," shouted Itch, peering down into the hollow inside of the trunk.

Buzz hurried up and joined Itch by the opening. Down below, inside the hollow trunk, was a space that contained, amongst other things, two lit-up glow-worms, a triple-decker wood sandwich, a collection of Beetles records, a carpet beater, some extra-silky bathing costumes and a sunflower smoothie maker.

"BINGO!" cried Itch with delight.

"At last," called up one of the glow-worms, smiling gratefully. "We thought we'd never get out of here."

"Thank goodness for you two!" cheered the second glow-worm.

The Fleatectives hurried down the inside of the trunk to join the glow-worms and the stolen stash.

"So this *tree trunk* is the burglar," marvelled Itch. "How are we going to carry it back to Sheriff Blatt?"

But at that second the Fleatectives heard the sound of approaching feet and a key twisting in a lock. The next second a narrow wooden door was pushed open and two figures stepped into the tree trunk room.

They were none other than . . . The Painted Lady and Crustman, with a swag bag each.

"THIS IS GETTING RIDICULOUS!" exclaimed Itch. "Now they're in THREE places at the same time."

But Buzz stepped forward and in one swift motion used his legs to rip off the large pieces of material stuck to the two new arrivals.

"Alfie and Old Ma Rocks!" gasped

Itch as the Painted Lady and Crustman costumes fell off the two dodgy-dealing spiders.

"These two have been carrying out all of the thefts, but their disguises convinced us that The Painted Lady and Crustman were the villains," said Buzz.

"So Sheriff Blatt's alibis were true!" said Itch, staring up in horror at the two huge and hairy spiders standing next to him.

**FLEATASTIC FACT:**

Tarantulas are very large and hairy and the biggest species can kill mice, lizards and birds!

"It's a brilliant scheme," declared Old Ma Rocks, "and we're big Bug notes in!" She and Alfie emptied their sacks. Out came a third glow-worm and a stack of stolen goods.

"ME LOVE MONEY! ME WANT MORE!" growled Alfie.

"So the dressing-up clothes we found in the shack didn't belong to any kids," said Itch. "They belonged to these two."

"And the strands of material we saw on the glow-worm wires came from these disguises!" nodded Buzz.

"But how did you know to come back

here?" asked Itch.

"It was when Sheriff Blatt coughed back at the Centipede Hotel. It reminded me of the noise we heard on Corn Street near the shadows tonight, and of the rumbling sound we heard on Yellow Seed Avenue. Those noises were the sound of Old Ma Rocks wheezing as she and Alfie ran away from the crime scenes."

Right on cue, Old Ma Rocks wheezed violently. Alfie gave her a powerful slap on the back, which only made her wheeze more. When she'd finished, she turned her blazing red eyes on the two Fleatectives.

"Shut the door, Alfie," she hissed.

Alfie kicked the narrow wooden door shut.

"Oh dear," said Itch.

"I knew you were imposters," wheezed

Old Ma Rocks, "and it's lucky we found you here before you went and told Sheriff Blatt or anyone else about our little adventures."

"I prefer to use the term crime spree," interrupted Itch.

"I threatened we'd crush you into flea paste," hissed Old Ma Rocks, as she and Alfie started moving towards Buzz and Itch. "Well, now we can turn that threat into reality!"

The two huge spiders towered over the Fleatectives.

"You really don't want to do this," shuddered Itch. "Flea paste tastes disgusting. Even on top-quality mud crackers!"

"Oh yes we do!" said Alfie.

"Let the flea paste production BEGIN!" cackled Old Ma Rocks.

# Can you find the
# three hidden glow-worms?

**Answers at the back of the book**

# CHAPTER 8

"This isn't good," trembled Itch as the spiders reached out to grab the Fleatectives.

"Prepare to be squished!" screeched Old Ma Rocks delightedly.

In a desperate bid to save himself, Itch lashed out with a useless kung-fu move that resulted in him kicking himself in the face. Luckily Buzz had a better idea. He snatched the disguises off the floor, grabbed Itch by his antennae and leapt into the air. The Fleatectives landed on the top of Alfie's head before they

bounced
up and on
to the inner
wall of the tree
trunk.

"This is no time for
dressing-up games!" shouted
Itch, pointing at the disguises held
in Buzz's claw.

"FORGET ABOUT THEM FOR A
MINUTE AND MOVE!" yelled Buzz.

"MASH THEM!" screamed Old Ma
Rocks.

Buzz and Itch raced up the inside wall
of the trunk with the gigantic spiders
hurtling up after them.

"My Aunt Mavis says that making
statements like '*Mash them!*' is the height
of bad manners!" screamed Itch.

"ME LOVE FLEA PASTE! ME

WANT MORE!" bellowed Alfie.

The Fleatectives jumped, sprung, sprinted (Itch pirouetted a couple of times) up the inner walls but the spiders were gaining on them fast. High up above was the hole at the top of the trunk.

"WE'LL OUTRUN YOU AND THEN WE'LL DEAL WITH YOU!" wheezed Old Ma Rocks as she kept pace with her son, her red eyes blazing with fury.

"I'm getting tired," groaned Itch. "I think I need a drinks break."

"Don't give up!" yelled Buzz. "We have to get to the top."

"What good is that?" shrieked Itch. "Even if we make it up there they'll just catch us on the way down outside!"

"KEEP GOING!" urged Buzz.

"We've nearly got them!" laughed Old Ma Rocks delightedly, scuttling up the inside wall of the trunk.

"ME LOVE FLEA PASTE AND MONEY! ME WANT MORE – MUCH MORE – OF BOTH!" howled Alfie.

The opening at the top was now only a short distance away, but Alfie suddenly caught one of Itch's legs in his own.

"Get off!" shrieked Itch, kicking Alfie's leg away.

As Buzz continued his ascent, he quickly tied the two disguises together.

"GRAB THE OTHER SIDE!" he shouted at Itch, flinging the material through the air.

"This isn't a fitting room!" complained Itch, catching it.

"Just pull it when we get to the top!"

commanded Buzz.

A few seconds later the Fleatectives reached the summit. Buzz jumped to the left and Itch jumped to the right, pulling the material taut between them across the top of the hole. The material stretched across the opening like a tightly spread sheet. As well as holding on to the material, the Fleatectives clung to the sides of the tree trunk so that they didn't fall down its outsides.

When Alfie and Old Ma Rocks reached the top a second later, they bashed straight into the stretched-out material and crashed backwards off it, falling at breakneck speed down inside the tree trunk and straight towards its floor.

"ME NOT LIKE THIS!" screamed Alfie, as he plummeted. "ME WANT

LESS OF THIS!"

When they hit the bottom the two spiders were both instantly knocked out cold. And there they lay on their backs, with their sixteen legs pointing up into the air.

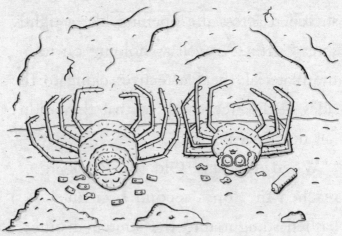

"YES!" cried Itch.

Buzz grabbed the material and quickly fashioned it into a loop. Grabbing it, the two Fleatectives jumped forward. Slowly and majestically, they floated down inside the tree trunk to its floor, using the tied-together disguises as a parachute. They landed next to the two silent spiders.

"That was AWESOME!" cheered the first glow-worm, doing a high five with Itch, body part to thorax.

"It *was* pretty good, wasn't it?" nodded Itch. "Lucky I thought of using the disguises to trap those two brutes and to create a parachute."

Buzz gave him a look.

"OK, OK," said Itch, "it was a joint effort."

"What are you going to do with these two crooks?" asked the second glow-worm.

"They're hairy and heavy," pointed out the third glow-worm.

"I have a great idea," replied Buzz. "Come with me."

He led Itch and the three glow-worms to the wheelbarrow he'd seen at the back of the shack. It was a very tight fit to get both spiders and all of the stolen booty into the wheelbarrow, but with a lot of squeezing and shoving it was achieved.

"If you all help us," said Buzz, "we'll be able to push this wheelbarrow back to Sheriff Blatt's office."

"No problem," grinned the first glow-worm. "It's the least we can do."

And so, an hour or so later, Buzz, Itch and the three glow-worms arrived at Sheriff Blatt's office. Luckily, he'd just got back from his card game at the Centipede Hotel.

"We present to you the glow-worm nabbers and all of the items they stole," said Itch proudly, "and we did all of the work ourselves."

"Apart from the work I did," replied Blatt.

"Er . . . you didn't do anything," said Itch.

"I did things in my mind, things no one saw, things that brought this case to a quick close," said Blatt.

"That's rubbish!" protested Itch. "The most you've done is sit in a chair!"

"My chairs are all designed for crime solving," replied Blatt.

"I have never heard such a—" started Itch.

"Leave it," said Buzz.

Itch sighed heavily and very reluctantly left it as Blatt emptied the two giant spiders into his office jail and locked the door.

Alfie and Old Ma Rocks came round a couple of hours later and started screaming and yelling to be released from Sheriff Blatt's jail, but the sheriff simply turned up the volume on *Midge Criminal Masterminds* and ignored them.

The next morning, Buzz, Itch and Sheriff Blatt set out for the south side of town to return all of the stolen items to their rightful owners.

"My triple-decker wood sandwich," trilled the termite, taking an enormous bite.

"We're going swimming!" shouted the father of the silkworm family when he spied their extra-silky bathing costumes.

"My carpet beater!" cheered the carpet moth, grabbing the beater and waving it through the air with delight.

"You're all very lucky to have a law enforcer like me around!" Sheriff Blatt informed everyone. "This 'S' on my back isn't there for nothing!"

Itch seethed at this comment, but he obeyed Buzz's request not to throw the sheriff into a rubbish bin. As the stolen glow-worms returned to their rightful places on Daffodil Place, Yellow Seed Avenue and Corn Street, Mayor Glug

showed up for a photo opportunity with the *Larva Town Lancet*. Itch and Sheriff Blatt fought each other to get closer to the mayor in the photo.

"I'd better get back to my office," said Mayor Glug, when everyone had drifted away. "I've got some relatives to eat."

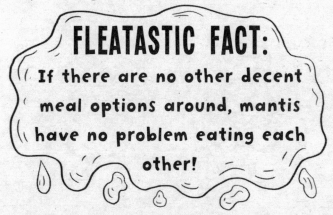

**FLEATASTIC FACT:**
If there are no other decent meal options around, mantis have no problem eating each other!

"And *I'd* better get back to taking some extra photos of myself for our brochure," said Itch.

"No problem," said Buzz. "How about we go home first and get a rabbit-bite to eat?"

"Nice idea," grinned Itch. "It will be a celebration meal! We've just cracked our second case and now I can't WAIT for our third one!"

# Can you match the the pairs?

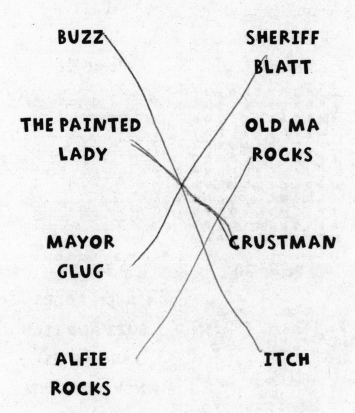

BUZZ

SHERIFF
BLATT

THE PAINTED
LADY

OLD MA
ROCKS

MAYOR
GLUG

CRUSTMAN

ALFIE
ROCKS

ITCH

Answers at the back of the book

## Page 12

```
Z J G X A Y I R F S U E
S P D R S J H U S T M L
T J E Q A A G E T J U R
H M S F D B N B S P D T
G F T D S R B A W Y Z Z
I Y R G R T U E Q W C O
L C J A V G Z V R Q U P
O A D L C F Z T M S G H
F G D I N C A K B C F G
T Y E T M L G L O W E D
A L A C N J B S C B Z L
M R V H V Y S T E A L M
```

## Page 41

START
FINISH

## Page 30

## Page 54

1. ALFIE ROCKS

2. BUZZ AND ITCH

3. BUG NOTES

4. NEVER KNOWN

WASTELAND

5. FLEATECTIVES

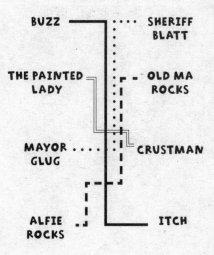
BUZZ ——————— SHERIFF BLATT

THE PAINTED LADY ——— OLD MA ROCKS

MAYOR GLUG ····· CRUSTMAN

ALFIE ROCKS ···· ITCH

# Have you read?

All the nectar in Larva Town
has gone missing!
The West Side bees say it's
the East Side bees, but are
either of them really to blame?
It's up to the Fleatectives
to find the culprit.

# CHAPTER 1

It was a warm early evening in Larva Town's West Side Wood and the sun was throwing lengthening shadows on the ground. A caterpillar was snoring on a nearby leaf, and a family of maggots were being made filthy by their mother.

It had been a quiet day for Buzz and Itch's newly founded Fleatectives Crime-Crushing Agency. In fact, every day was quiet, as the number of cases they'd managed to pick up so far was . . . zero.

Itch was jumping across an area of smooth mud and muttering to himself.

Buzz looked up from last month's copy of *Insect Crime Monthly* (this month's had mysteriously gone missing). "What are you doing?" he asked his crime-crushing partner.

"Trying to fly," replied Itch.

"How many times do I have to tell you?" Buzz sighed, wiggling his antennae with frustration. "We're FLEAS. We don't have wings so we don't fly!"

"But I could be the first flying flea," replied Itch, looking hopeful. He was about to carry on with his flying project when two thorax-shaking shrieks rang through the wood.

"THE WEST SIDE HIVE NEVER TAKES MORE THAN IT NEEDS!"

"THE EAST SIDE HIVE WOULD NEVER DREAM OF STEALING!"

"What's that about?" asked Itch.

"We'd better go and investigate," replied Buzz.

The two of them hurried past a line of twigs and arrived at the source of the outburst. Two female honeybees were standing compound-eye to compound-eye on a jagged pebble, bawling at each other.

One had the light brown stripes of the local West Side hive bees. The other's stripes were darker, indicating she was from the East Side hive.

"THIEF!"

"ROBBER!"

"Ladies, LADIES!" exclaimed Buzz, striding over and placing his tiny frame between them. "What seems to be the problem?"

"Not that it's any of your business," snapped the West Side bee, looking down at him, "but the entire West Side of town is totally nectar free; there's not a drop of it anywhere. And that's because *her* lot from the East Side have been encroaching into our air space and taking what's NOT THEIRS!"

"That is absolute RUBBISH!" hissed her opponent. "The only reason I've travelled here from the East Side is because we have no nectar in *our* zone. We reckon it's the West Side posse who have filched the lot."

"How DARE you!" screamed the West Sider.

"OH I DARE!" hollered the East Sider.

"Maybe they've been taking *each other's* nectar," suggested Itch.

# Who stole the nectar?

### Read
# CASE OF THE STOLEN NECTAR
## to find out!

(OFFICIAL FLEATECTIVE BROCHURE PHOTOS)

BUZZ

ITCH